Maremaid

A Pony's Tale

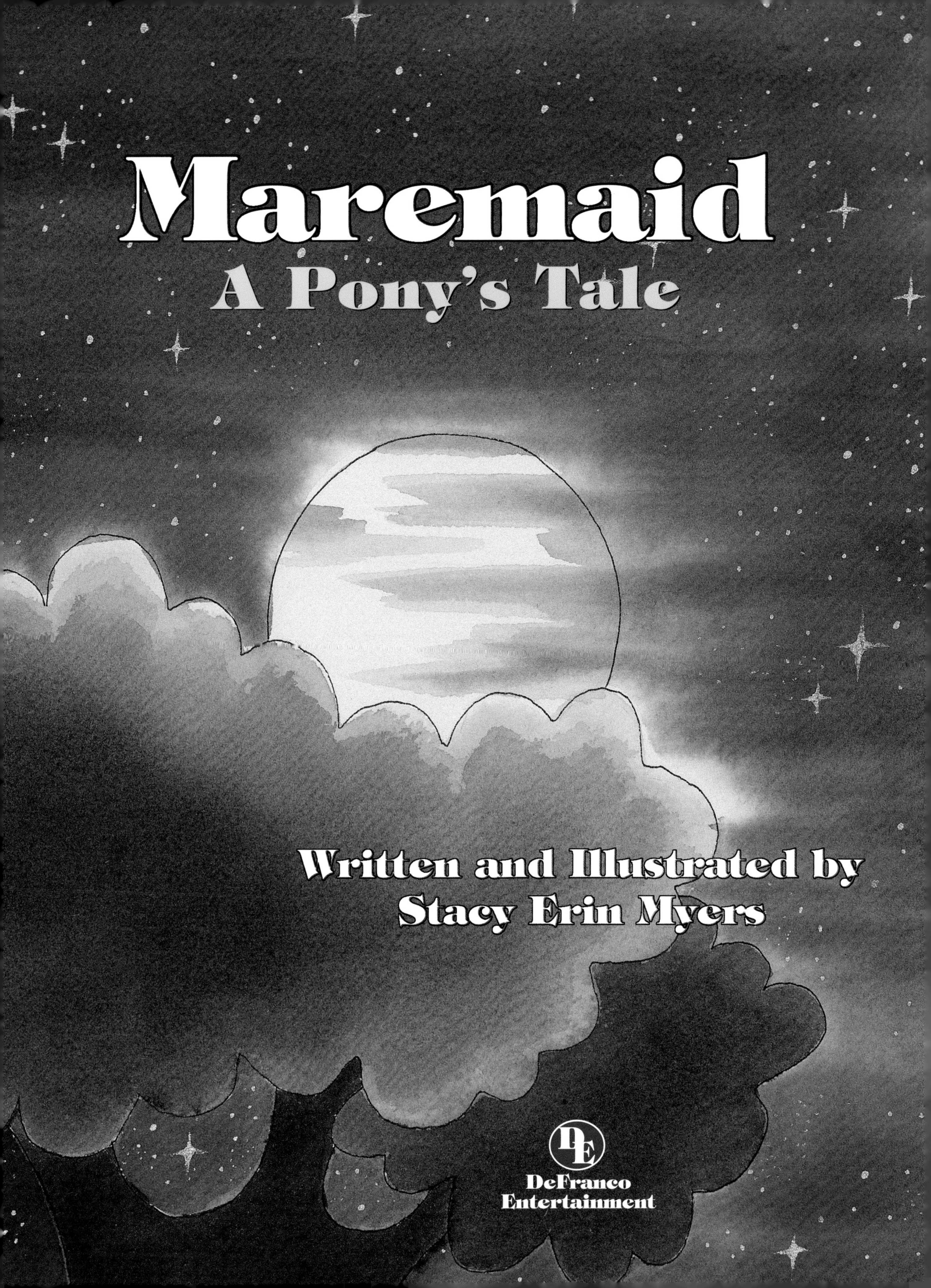

Written and Illustrated by
Stacy Erin Myers

DeFranco
Entertainment

Maremaid
A Pony's Tale

Written and Illustrated by
Stacy Erin Myers

DeFranco Entertainment
P.O. Box 1425
Thousand Oaks, CA 91358

First Edition

Edited by Kathy Kirkland and Robrt Pela
Graphic design by Lisa Sutton
Printed and bound in Singapore

The paintings for this book were done in watercolor and rapidograph.

Maremaid: A Pony's Tale/Written and illustrated by Stacy Erin Myers
Summary: Toy pony ride wishes to be a real pony and meets an angel
in an unlikely place.
ISBN (1-929845-11-1)
Library of Congress Card Number: 00-100400
(1. Maremaid/Fiction) First Title

10 9 8 7 6 5 4 3 2 1

A special smile and thanks to

Tessa, Elyse and Beau

for their encouragement and vision.

And to Tony for making my wish come true.

Once upon a time, a lonely 25-cent pony ride named Derbie sat at the end of a pier. A big fire had destroyed the pier long ago, leaving only echoes of children's laughter to fill the air of this lonely place.

Across the bay was a beautiful island where ponies ran free, wild flowers grew and tall grass blew in the wind. All that was left for the 25-cent pony ride was the island to dream about.

And the wish to be a real pony...

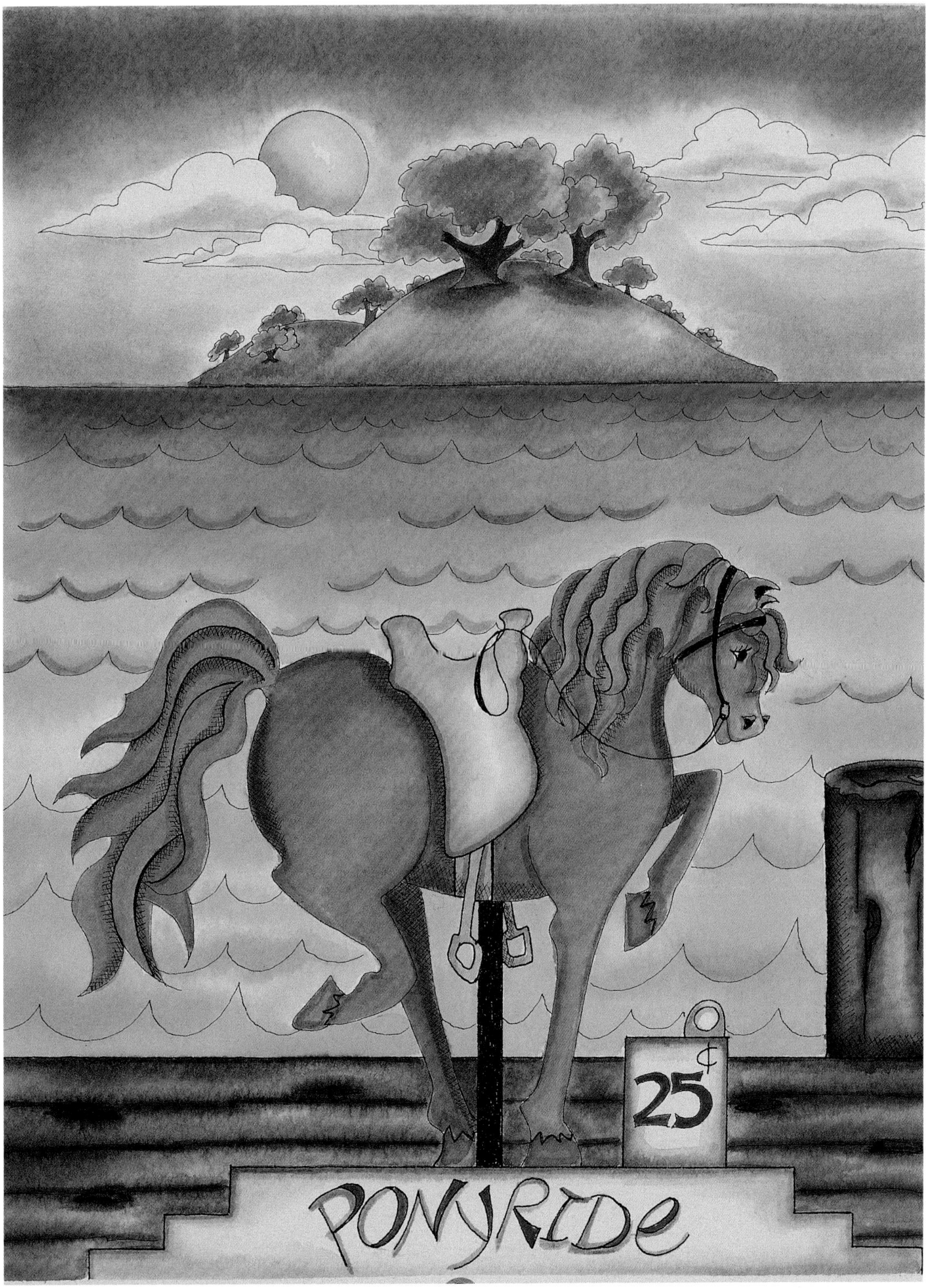
25¢
PONYRIDE

At night, Derbie gazed out into the midnight-blue sky filled with silvery stars, the little island seemed so far away.

She thought if just one of the beautiful stars that lit up her lonely nights fell across the sky, she would make a wish:

To swim across the bay and become a real pony...

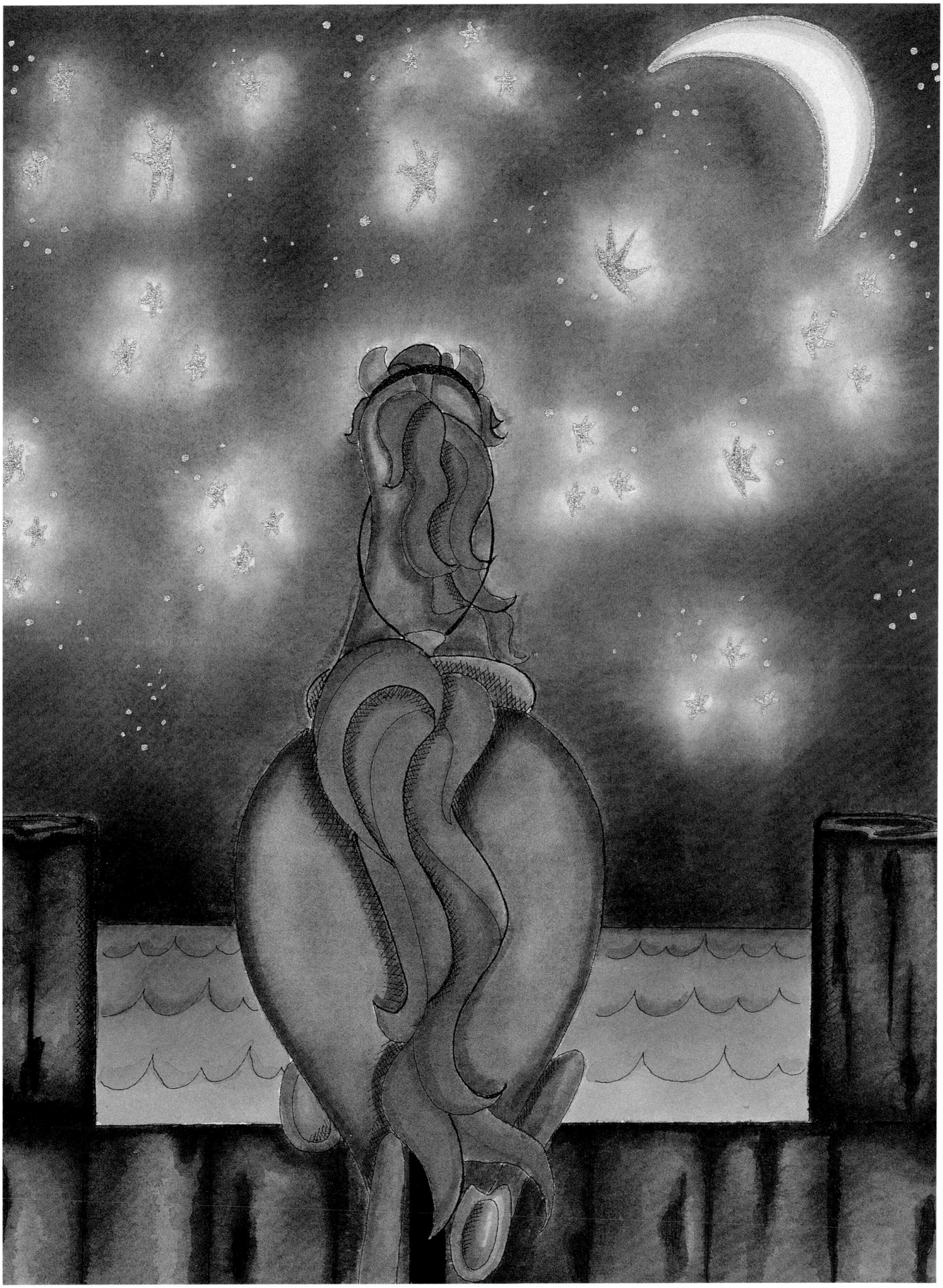

One evening, Derbie became very sad. All her hopes of becoming a real pony seemed impossible.

The sky was dark with rain clouds, and the wind was so brisk, even her plastic fur coat couldn't keep her warm heart from breaking.

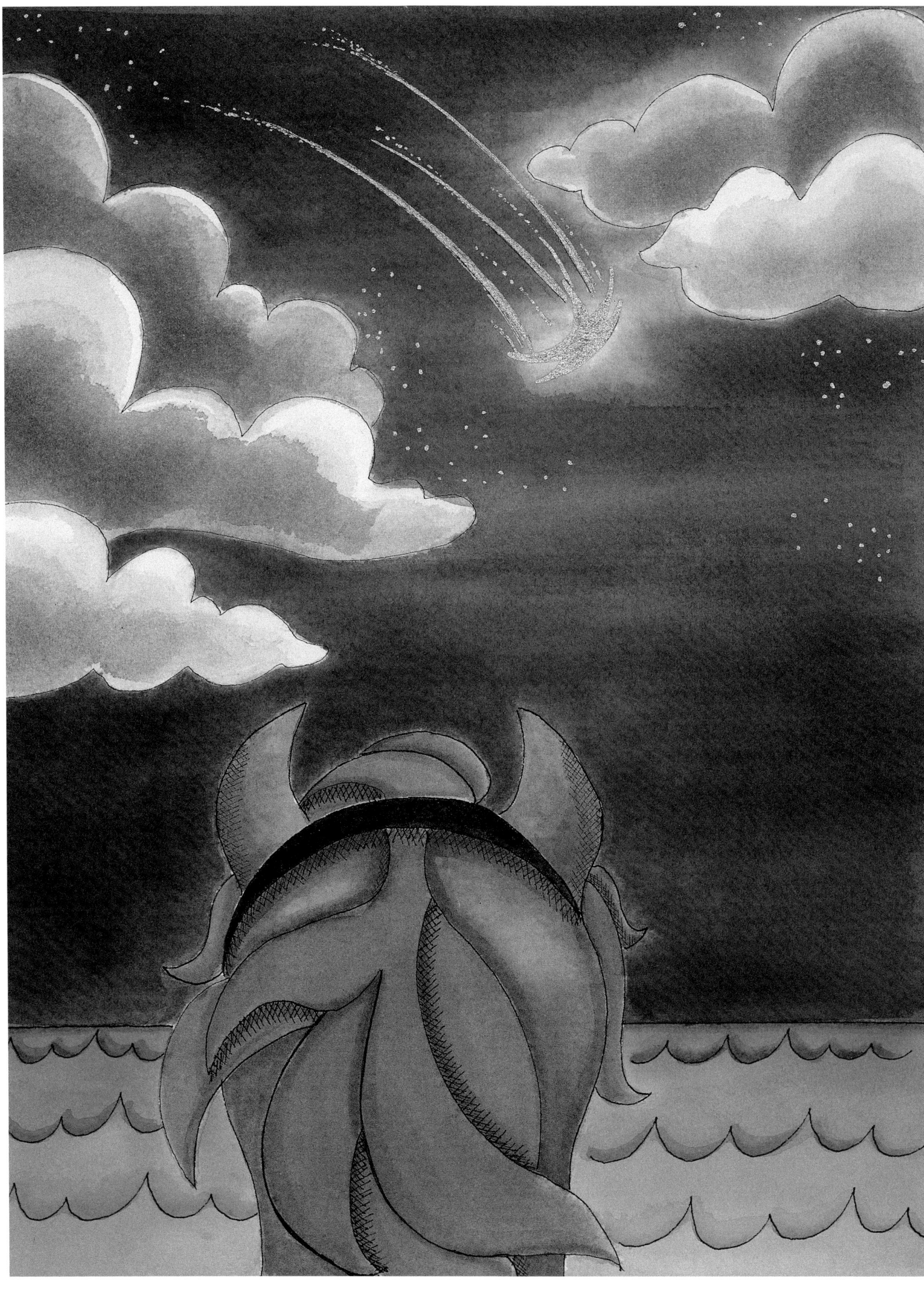

Suddenly, the clouds parted and the biggest, brightest star shot through the sky! Derbie, in an instant, made her wish.

"Please, oh please, bright falling star, let me swim swiftly to the island that's just too far!"

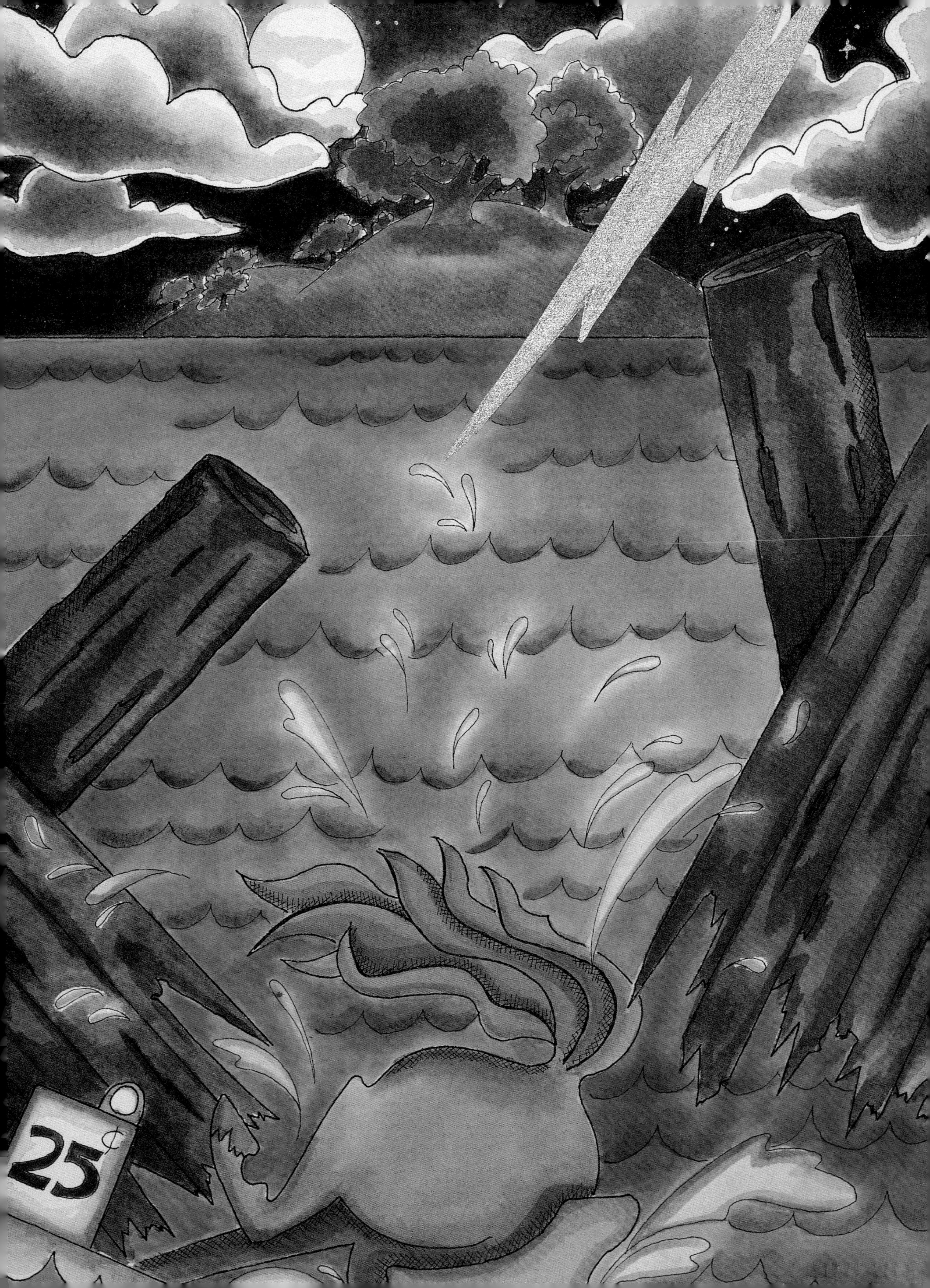
25¢

At that moment, a loud clap shook the pier and a bolt of lightning split it in two, sending the pony ride into the bay, where she sank fast to the dark below.

And in the distance there came a rumbling thunder, and Derbie's falling star splashed into the bay.

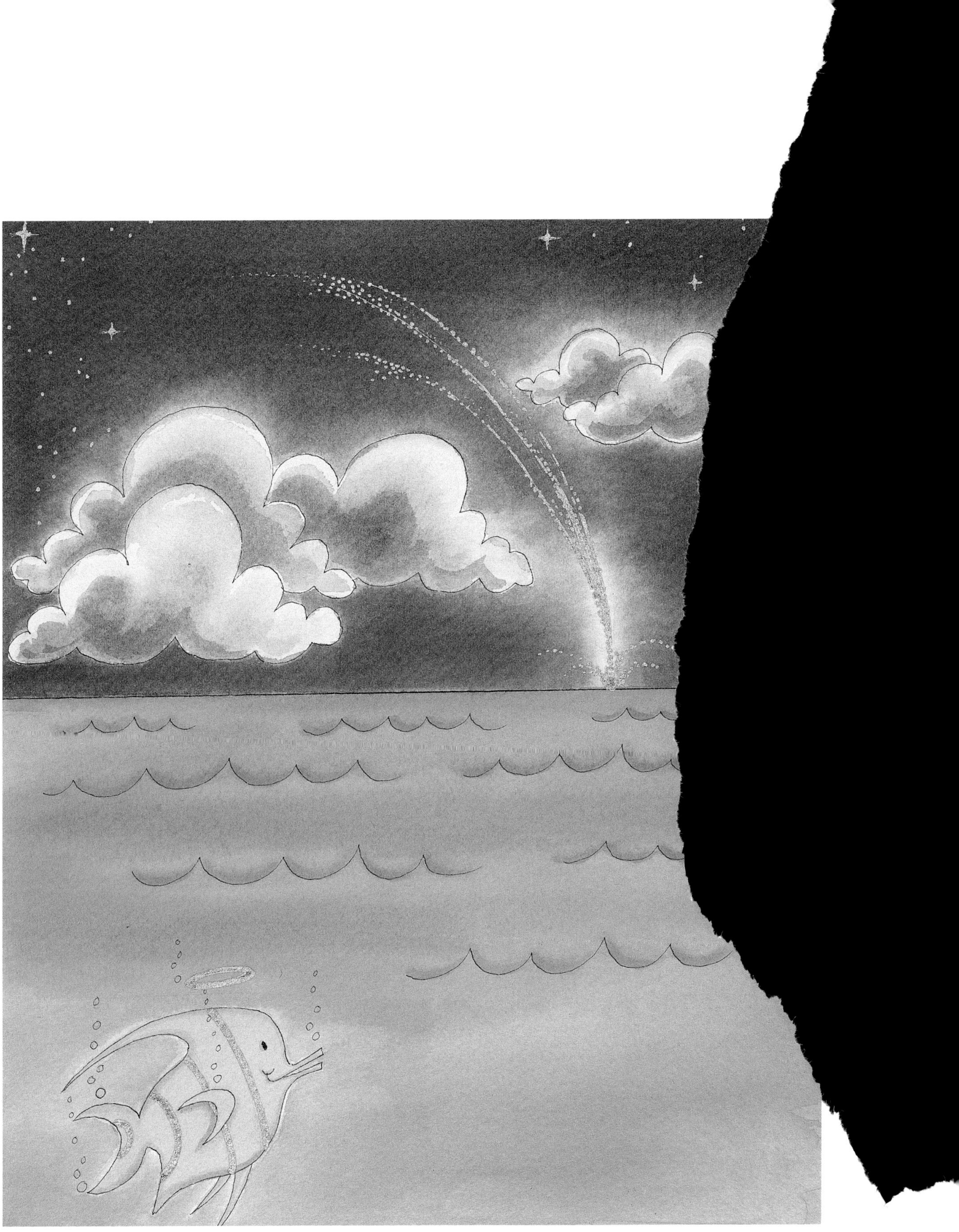

sled and confused, Derbie opened her
bubbles swirling around everywhere,
oup of the funniest-looking
rounding

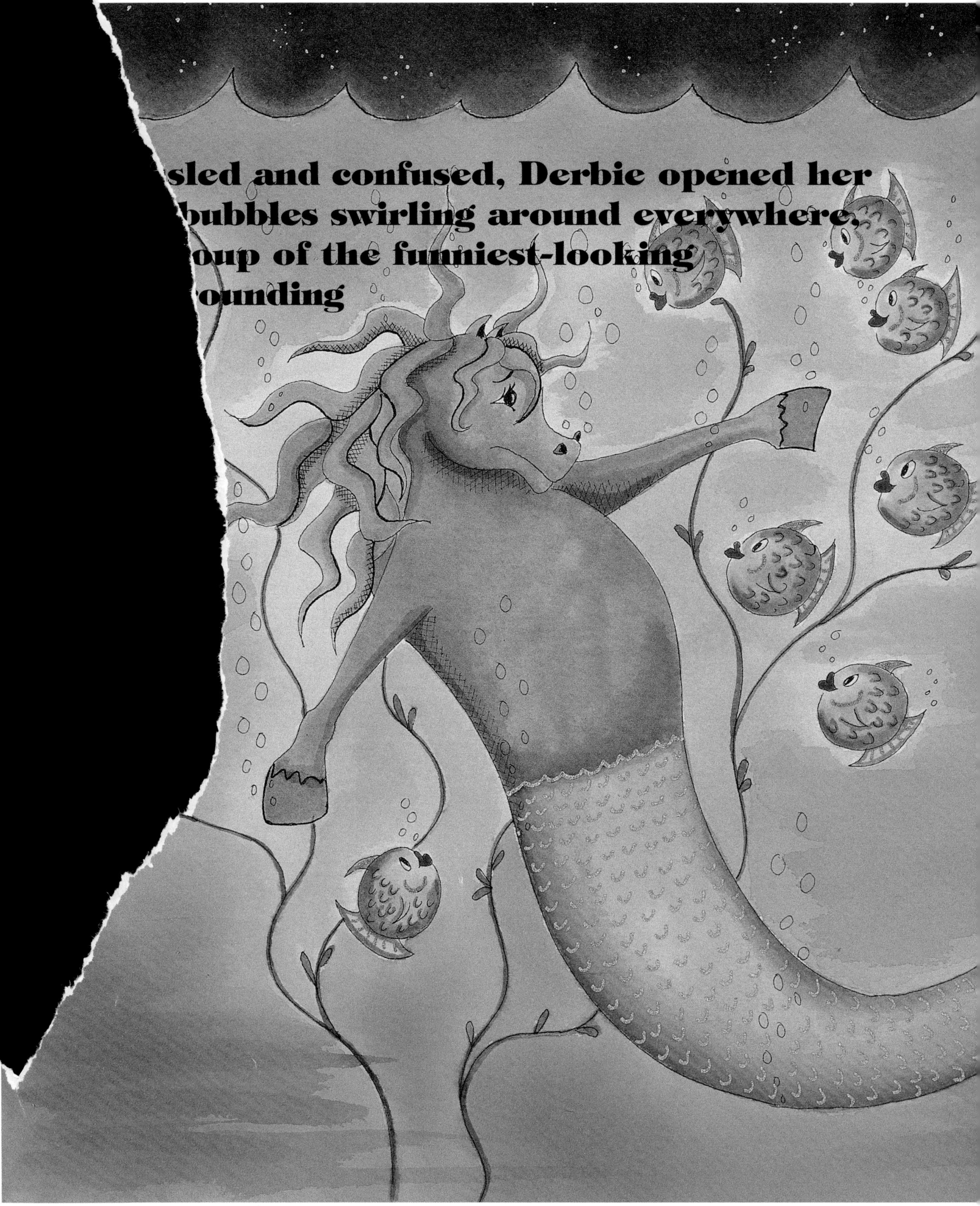

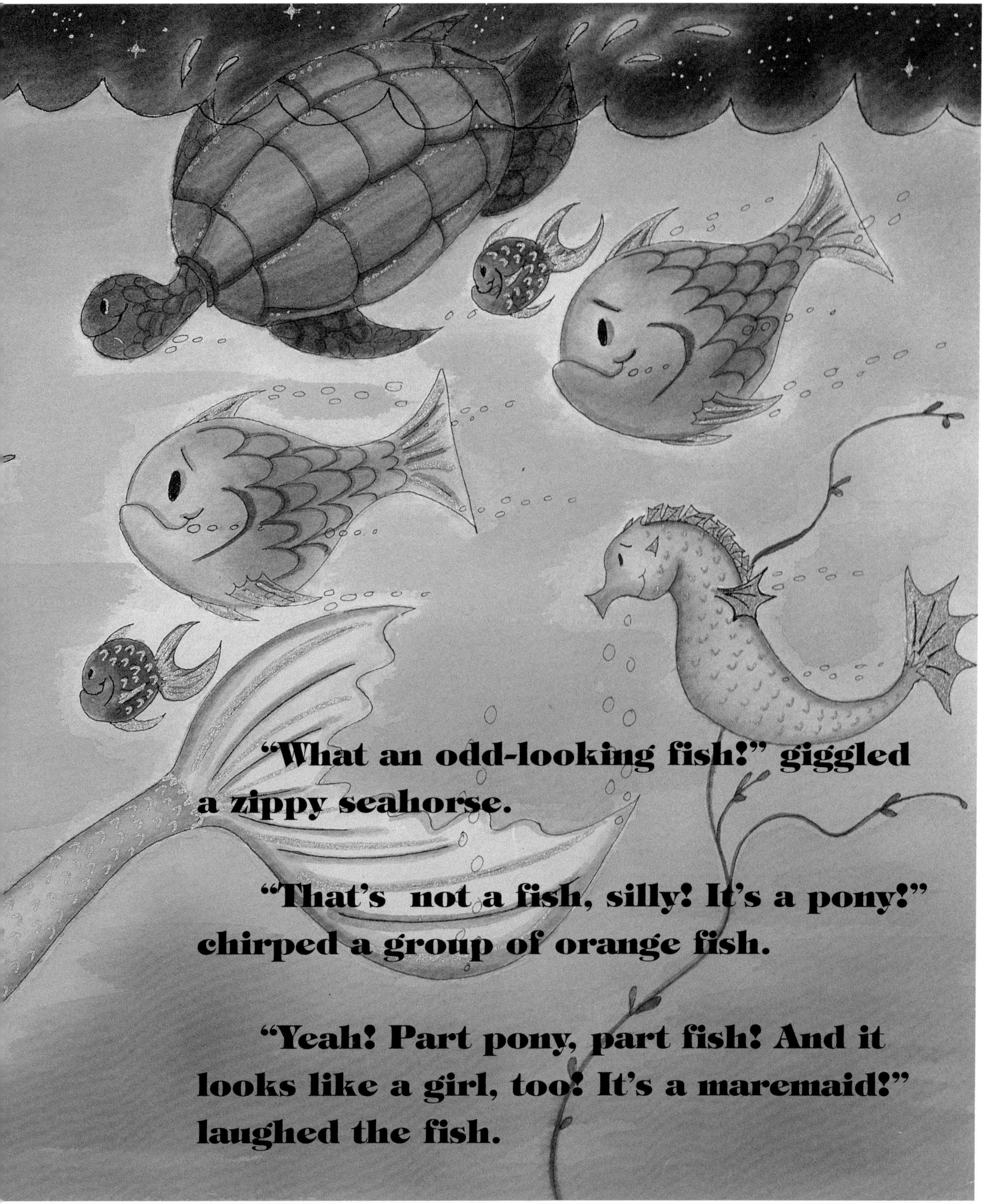

"What an odd-looking fish!" giggled a zippy seahorse.

"That's not a fish, silly! It's a pony!" chirped a group of orange fish.

"Yeah! Part pony, part fish! And it looks like a girl, too! It's a maremaid!" laughed the fish.

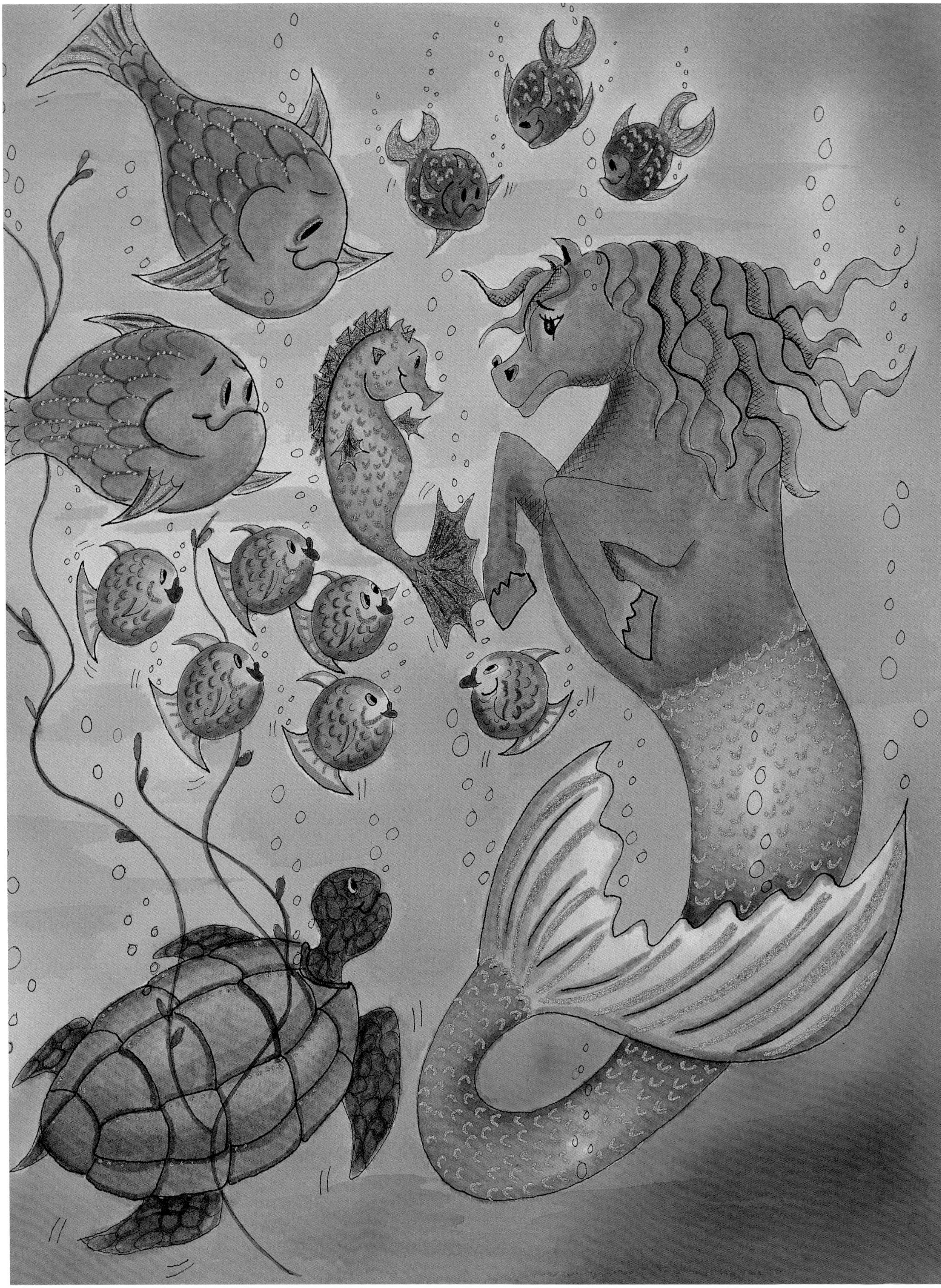

Derbie tried to explain to the colorful group of fish that she simply made a wish on a falling star.

She'd wished to be able to swim across the bay and become a real pony.

"Now look at me!" she cried. "I have scales and a tail! I look like a fish!

This isn't what I wished for!"

The fish grew sad for this unfortunate "maremaid," and gathered close to comfort her, when all of a sudden the fish became still, and a beautiful angel fish appeared!

"My name is Angelish, and I am your guardian angel fish!" she said. "I'm to watch over you and grant you a second wish, but first you must realize why your wish didn't come true to your liking..."

The maremaid hung her pretty head low. "I don't know why this happened! I wished to swim across the bay and become a real pony, but I got a fin instead!"

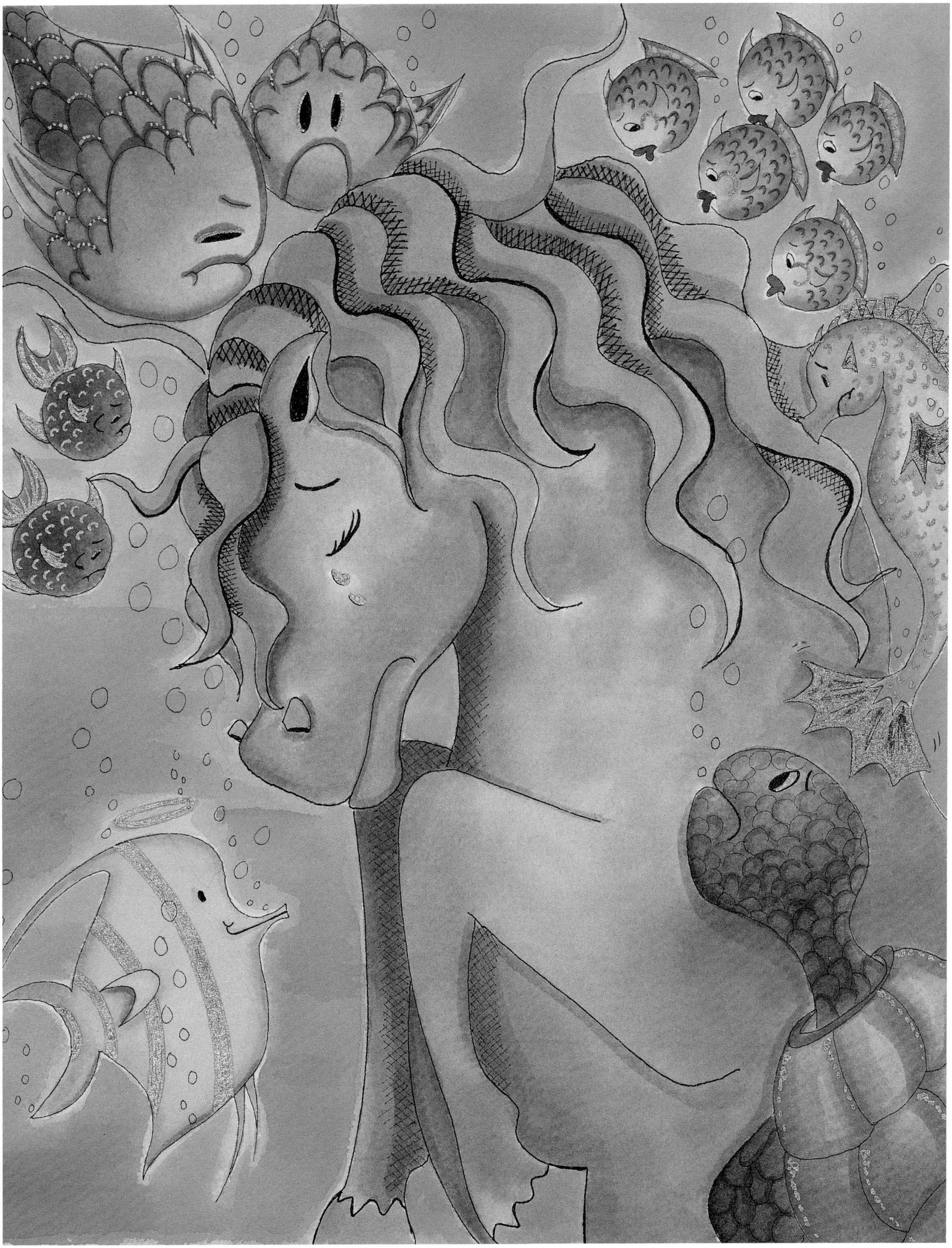

"Oh, no," said Angelish. "You got exactly what you first wished for!

You see, a real horse could never swim that far across the bay to the island, but a *seahorse* could!

Your wish was granted: You are now a maremaid. You should never make two wishes on one falling star!"

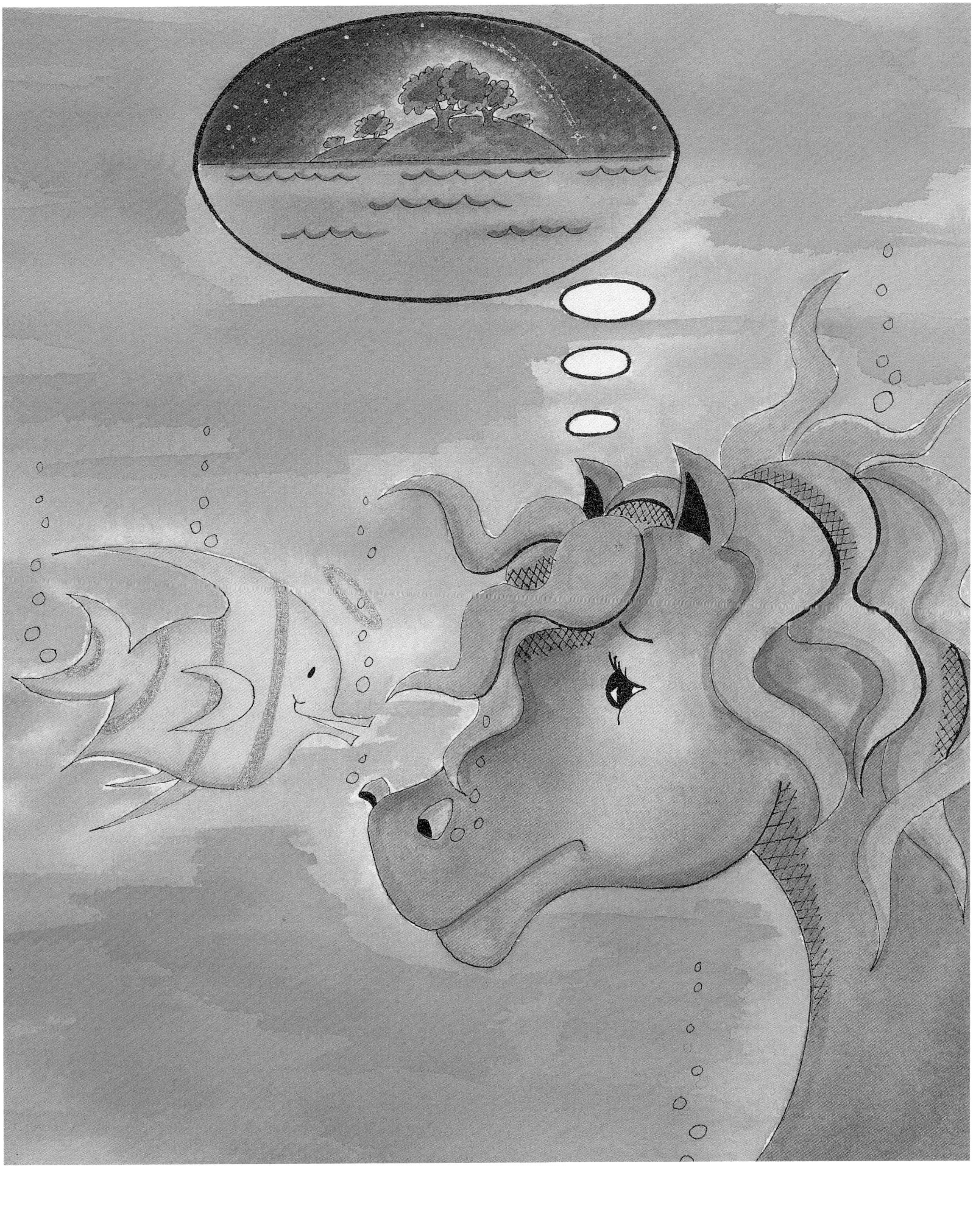

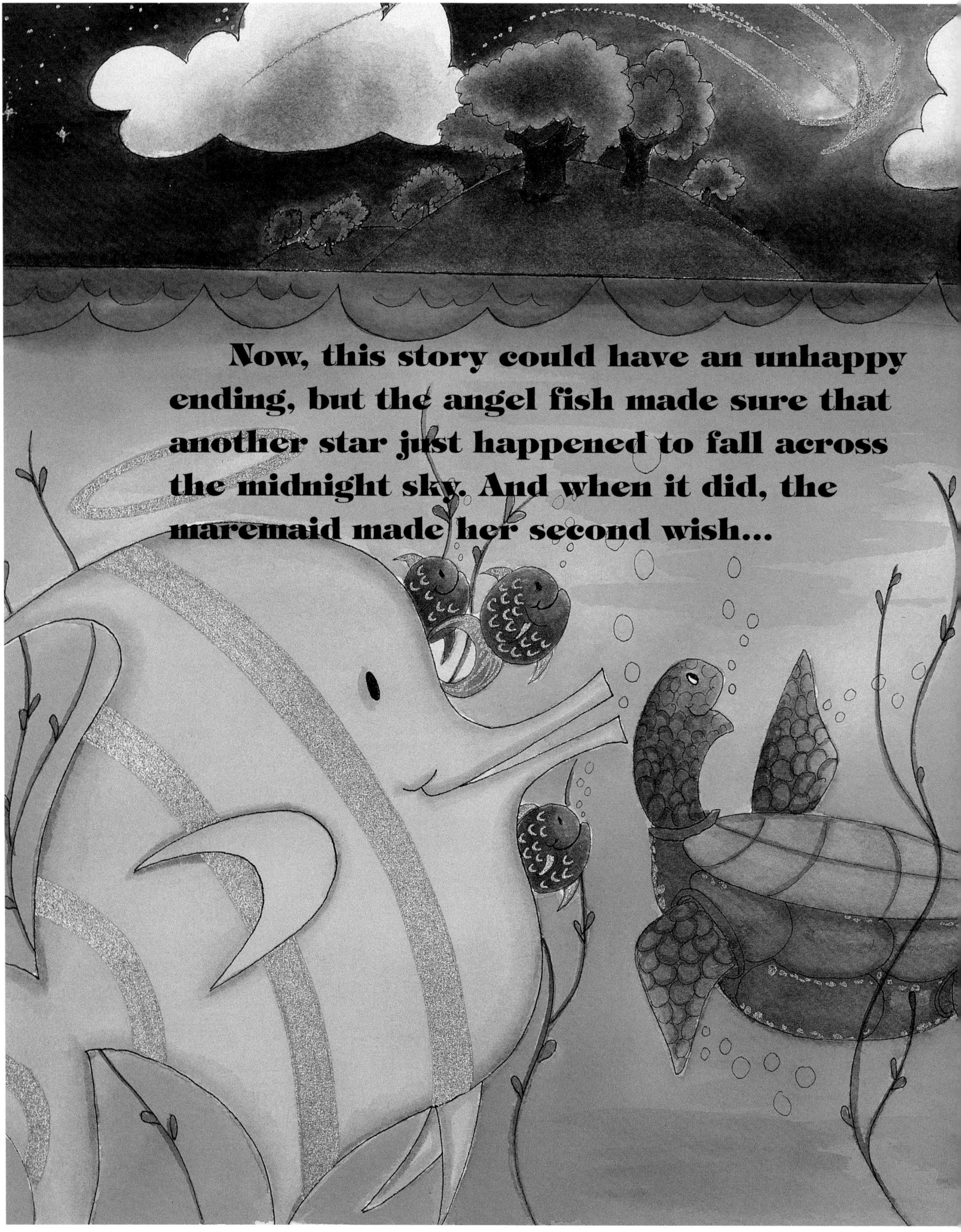

Now, this story could have an unhappy ending, but the angel fish made sure that another star just happened to fall across the midnight sky. And when it did, the maremaid made her second wish...

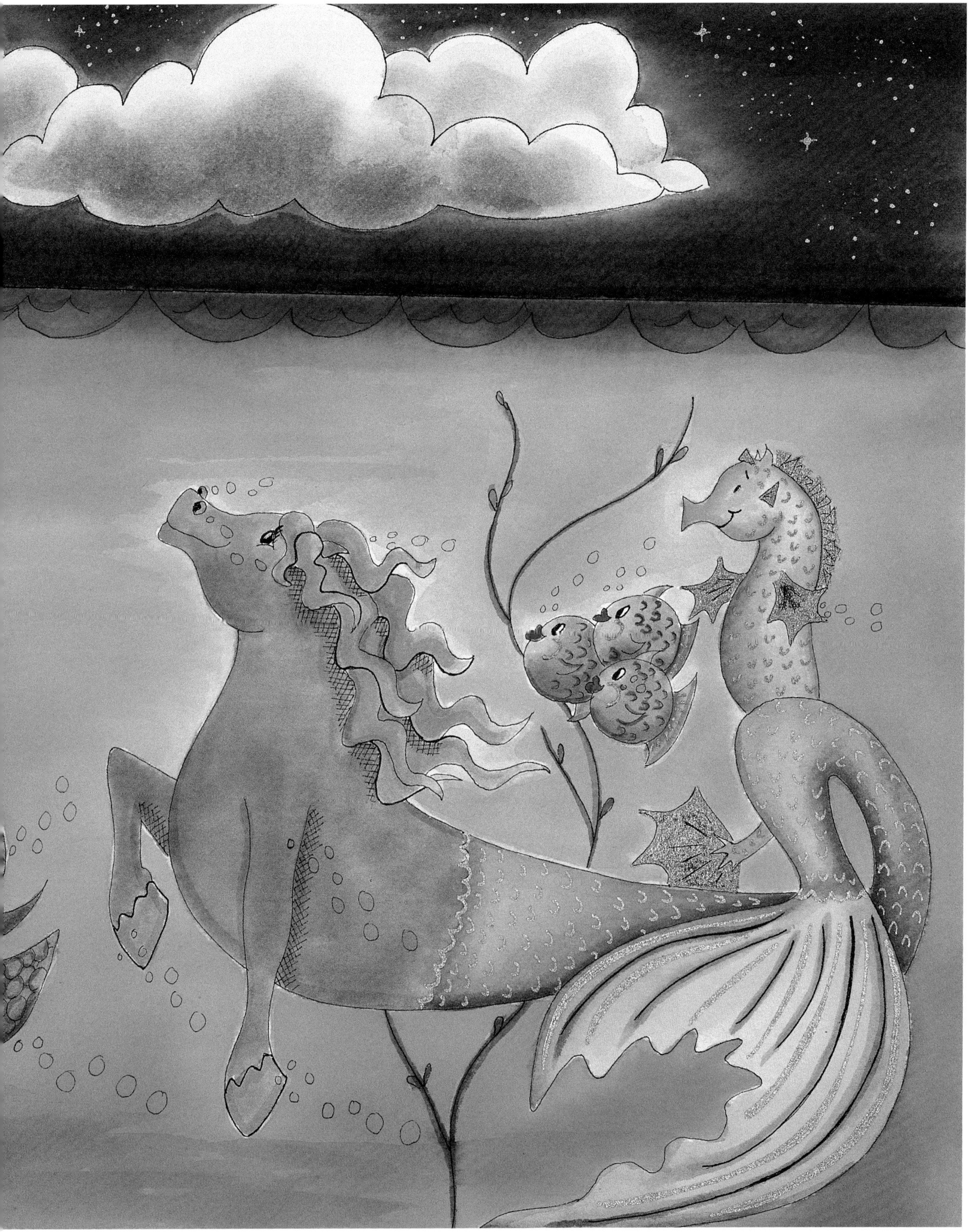

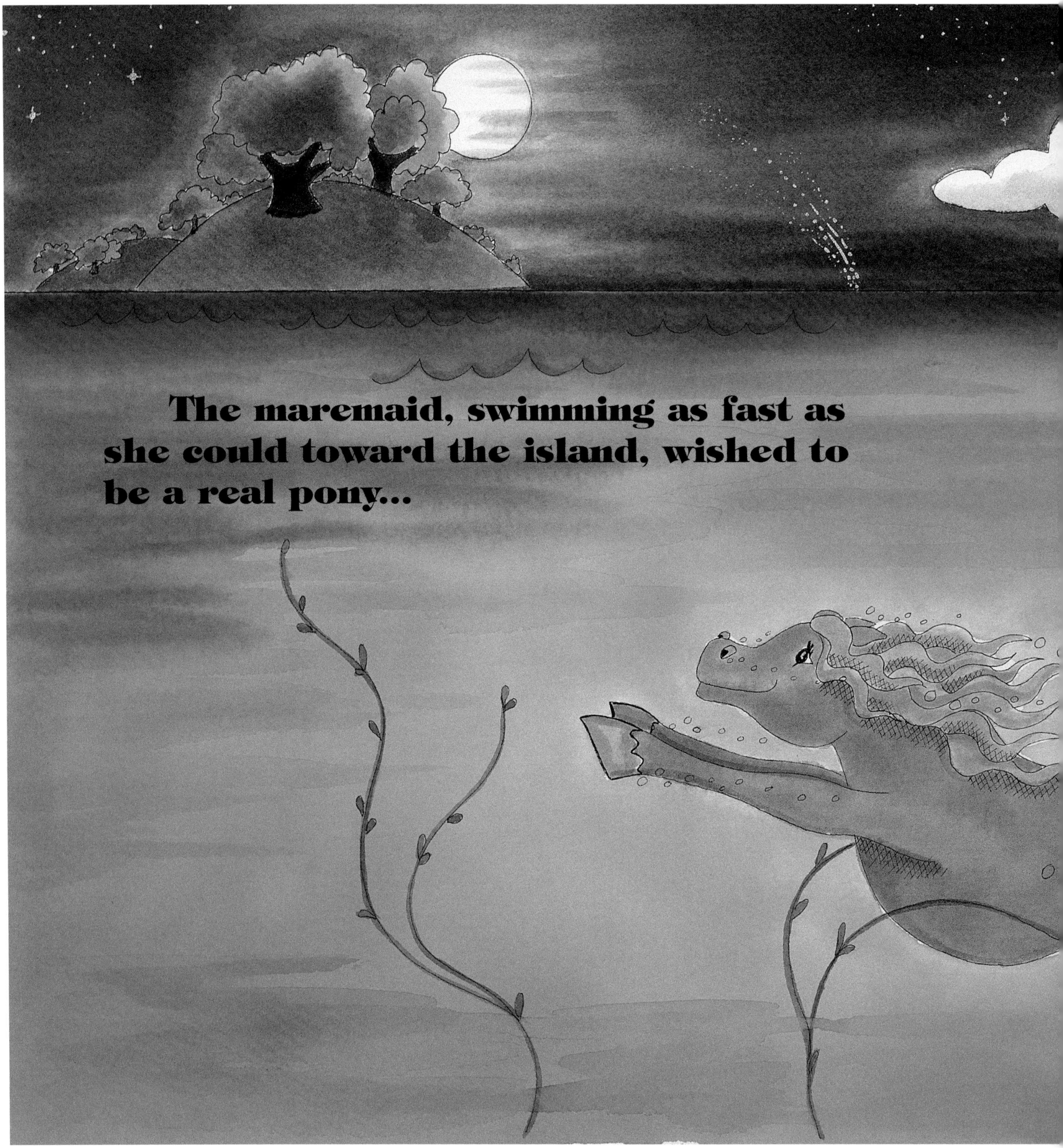

The maremaid, swimming as fast as she could toward the island, wished to be a real pony...

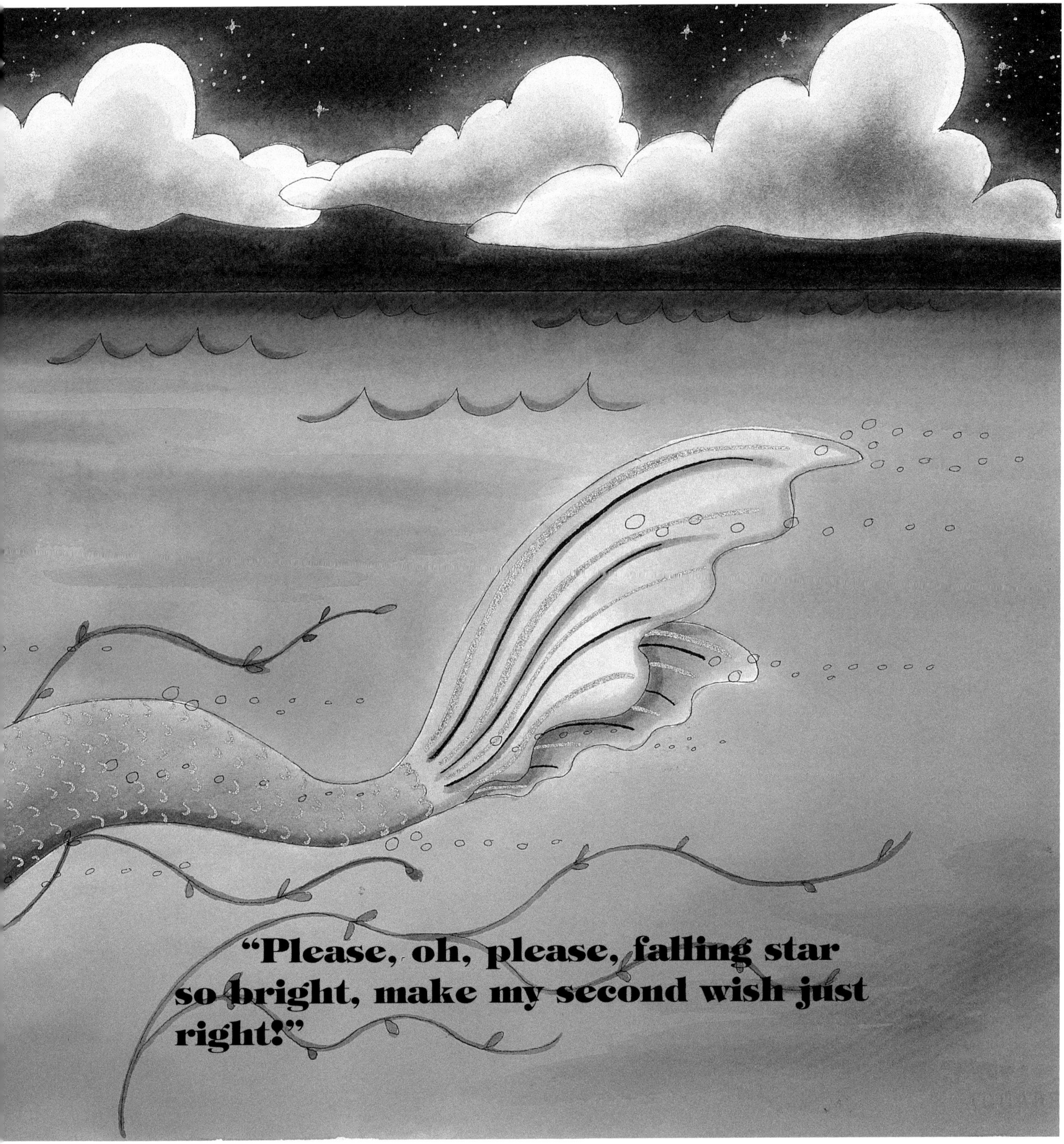

"Please, oh, please, falling star so bright, make my second wish just right!"

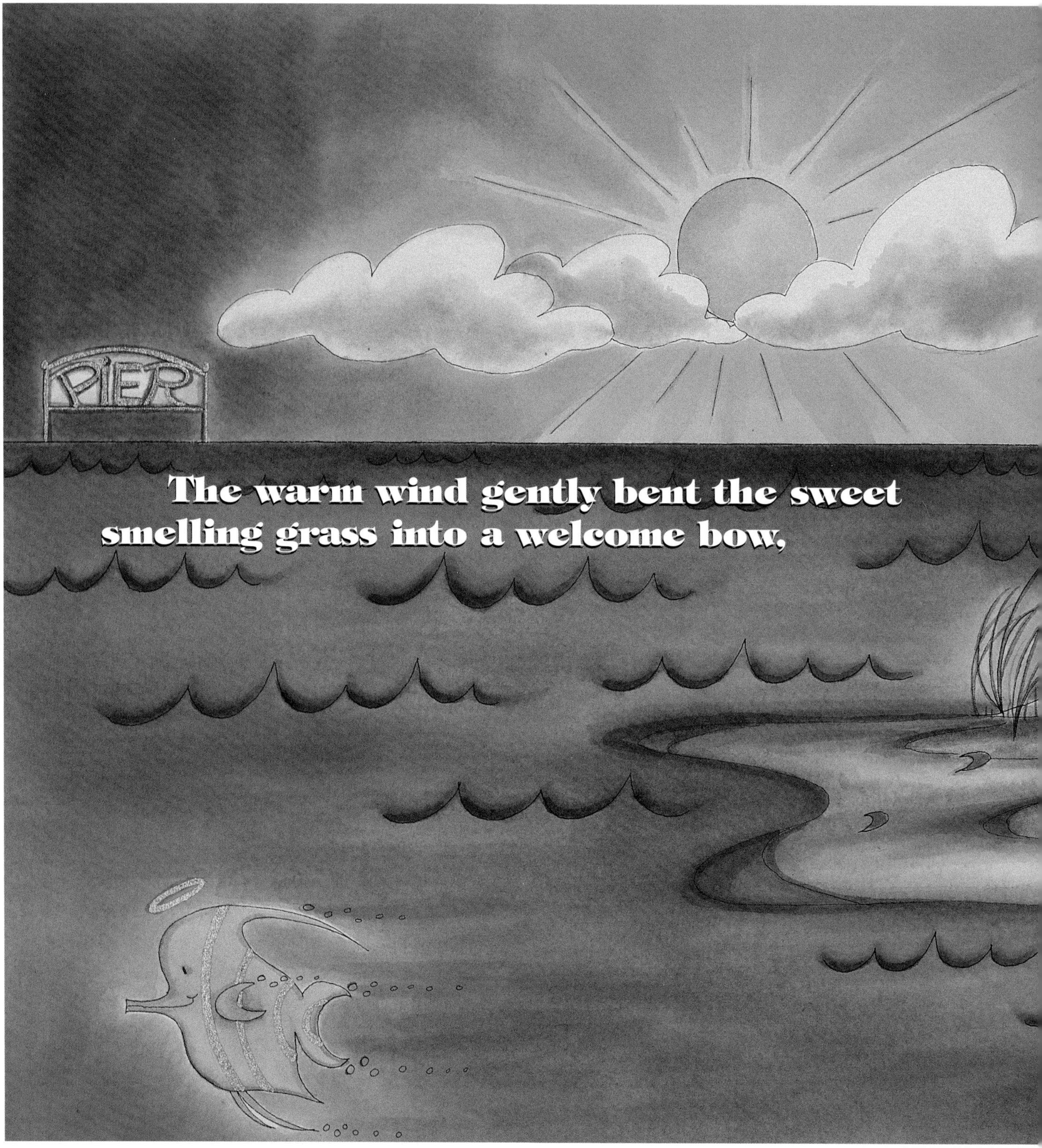
PIER

The warm wind gently bent the sweet smelling grass into a welcome bow,

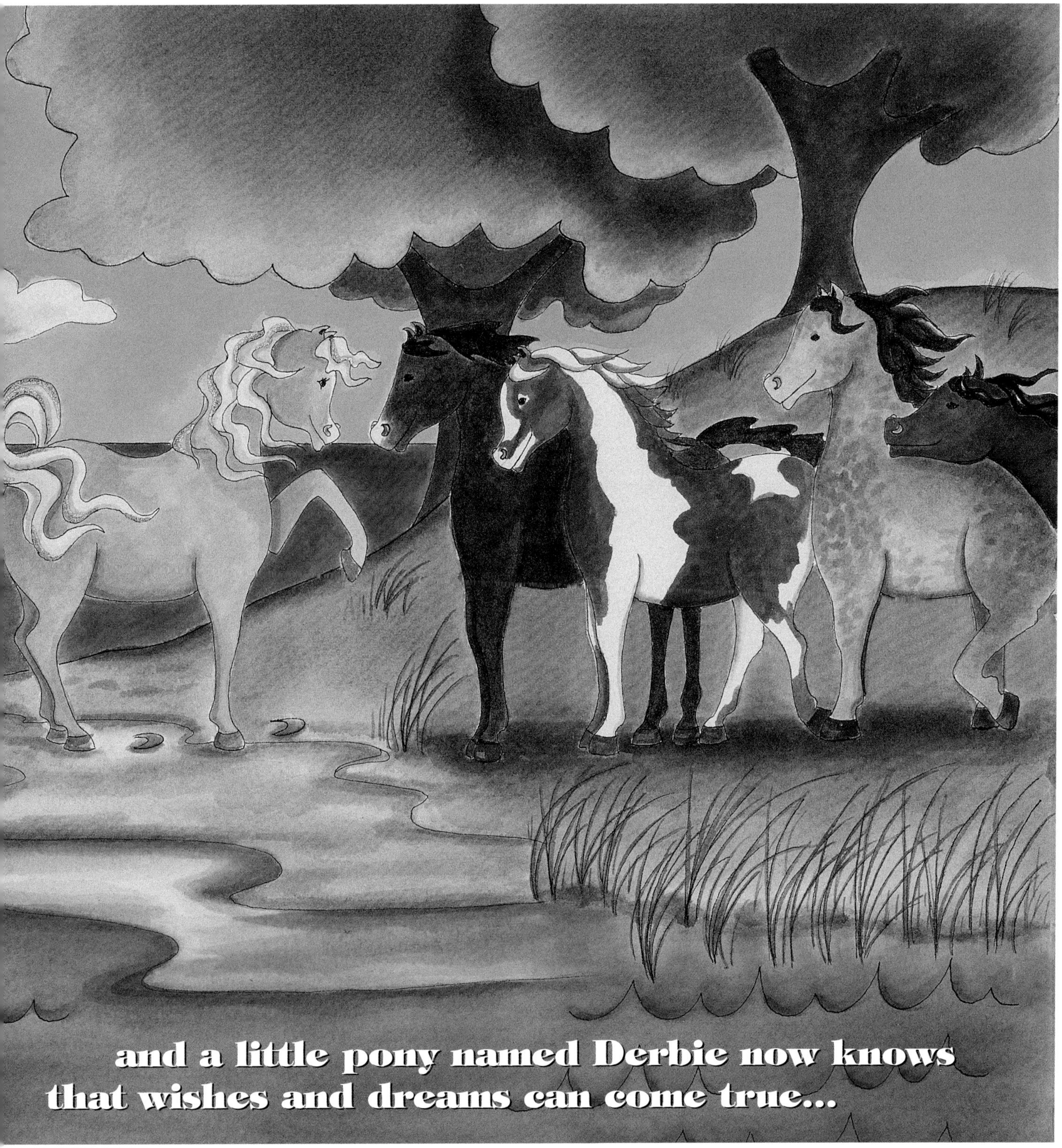

and a little pony named Derbie now knows
that wishes and dreams can come true...

The island across the bay was not so far away...

Dedicated to all the forgotten pony rides
across the land, who let us dream
our dreams the old-fashioned way.

The End